For Lyla
from Emmy + Jay

MERMAID
SCHOOL

BY
JOANNE STEWART WETZEL

ILLUSTRATED BY
JULIANNA SWANEY

ALFRED A. KNOPF 🐕 NEW YORK

I brush my hair. I shine my tail.
I cannot stop to play.
It's time to leave for Mermaid School.
Today is my first day.

When I arrive, there's no one here
That I have met before.
But I can make new friends at school.
I'm always glad for more.

A boy is hiding by the kelp.
I think he's feeling shy.
"Hello. I'm Molly. What's your name?"
"I'm Squirt" is his reply.

"Why are you hiding?"
  I ask Squirt.
"There's no one here I know."
"Well, we can fix that in a flash.
  Let's go and say hello."

Our teacher, Miss Marina, calls,
"Please line up in a queue
And follow me inside our reef.
I'll show you what to do."

"Your cubbies have your names on them.
Your tailpacks go inside.
If you forget to take them home,
They'll float off with the tide."

Miss Marina hands out seashells.
We count them one by one.
We add and then we take away,
Until we're back to none.

For art class we use shells again
To make things we can wear.
We string them into necklaces.
I braid some in my hair.

To memorize the alphabet,
We sing the A-B-Seas.
Soon we'll know each letter's sound
And learn to read with ease.

Our music teacher comes in next.
Her name's Miss Lorelei.
Her trumpetfish accompany
Our notes from low to high.

And when they play a faster tune,
Her drum fish join the band.
We swirl our tails and, hand in hand,
We dance across the sand.

It's time for recess. Let's go play!
We check out everything.

Squirt builds a row of sand castles—
I ride the great kelp swing.

We shoot up in a waterspout.
Then we play hide-and-seek.

When I was "It," I found them all—
And no, I didn't peek.

There's clamburgers for lunch today,
Along with seaweed pie.
And frozen salt pops for dessert!
There's nothing I don't try.

We hurry back for Circle Time.
And as our food digests,

We play a game.
We sing a song.

Then comes the very best.

Our teacher reads a story that
She calls a fantasy.
Of boys and girls who have no tails
And can't breathe undersea.

Miss Marina sticks a starfish
By each name on her chart.
She says, "Let's sing 'The Goodbye Song'
Before we all must part."

I can't believe it's time to go.
How can the day be done?
The hours here have just flown by,
'Cause Mermaid School is fun!

The tide comes in, the tide goes out,

And mermaid school now ends.

Tomorrow we will all be back

to play with our new friends.

Goodbye

For Marilyn Miller and all the Naiads
we swam with at ASU –J.S.W.

For my mom and dad,
who taught me to swim –J.S.

THIS IS A BORZOI BOOK PUBLISHED BY ALFRED A. KNOPF

Text copyright © 2018 by JoAnne Stewart Wetzel

Jacket art and interior illustrations copyright © 2018 by Julianna Swaney

All rights reserved. Published in the United States by Alfred A. Knopf, an imprint of Random House Children's Books,
a division of Penguin Random House LLC, New York.

Knopf, Borzoi Books, and the colophon are registered trademarks of Penguin Random House LLC.

Visit us on the Web! rhcbooks.com

Educators and librarians, for a variety of teaching tools, visit us at RHTeachersLibrarians.com

Library of Congress Cataloging-in-Publication Data

Names: Wetzel, JoAnne, author. | Swaney, Julianna, illustrator.

Title: My first day at Mermaid School / by Joanne Stewart Wetzel ; illustrated by Julianna Swaney.

Description: First edition. | New York : Alfred A. Knopf, 2018. | Summary: Molly enjoys her first day at Mermaid School,
where she makes new friends, learns new things, and hears a story about children with no tails.

Identifiers: LCCN 2017021582 (print) | LCCN 2017037411 (ebook) | ISBN 978-0-399-55716-3 (trade) |
ISBN 978-0-399-55717-0 (lib. bdg.) | ISBN 978-0-399-55718-7 (ebook)

Subjects: | CYAC: Stories in rhyme. | First day of school—Fiction. | Schools—Fiction. | Mermaids—Fiction. | Friendship—Fiction.

Classification: LCC PZ8.3.W49997 (ebook) | LCC PZ8.3.W49997 My 2018 (print) | DDC [E]—dc23

MANUFACTURED IN CHINA

July 2018   10 9 8 7 6 5   First Edition

Mermaid School Handbook

Pets: School is no place for your family pet. Please leave your dogfish, catfish, or seahorse at home.

New Students: If you meet a new mermaid swimming by, ask her name and tell her yours. It's a great way to make friends.

Help Keep Our Planet Blue: Protect the living creatures that make our planet beautiful. Be careful swimming near fragile corals, jellyfish, or sea anemones. Give passing schools of fish the right-of-way.

Practice Playground Courtesy: Wait in line to take your turn to ride the great kelp swing.

Make sure no one lives in a cave before you try to hide in it when playing hide-and-seek. Many caves in our neighborhood are the homes of octopi, who may squirt ink on uninvited guests.

The humpback whales that migrate past our school have asked that students stop tickling their stomachs when they swim overhead.

After-School Activities

Tuesday: Choir. Sing in our school choir! Our world-famous music teacher, Miss Lorelei, whose enchanting voice became legendary when she sang to ships sailing on the Rhine River, will conduct.

Thursday: Water Ballet. Join the Mermaid School Synchronized Swim Team and learn how to do such figures as the Oyster, the Dolphin, and the Torpedo.